"BEAR"

by Robert Cullen

4

One thousand years before the enslaved Israelites made their exodus, the Egyptians performed acts of circusry in their precarious kingdom. Thickmiddled women in their tied off robes and ear rings and striped neck collars bent back, breasts bared to the sky, sundarkened contortionists and balancers in the first days of recorded history.

Were they watching what had become of their trade on that night? He came out from the portable toilet wringing his hands and watching the tent city erected on the esplanade. In his thirty one years he stood rugged, murmuring little things to himself like an old man. Were you there with him you might have heard him say something like Well, it's showtime. Or Here we go Woodard.

He jogged over to the tent rear in his jeans and workshirt and stepped inside where stood the cast and crew, the contortionists in their tiny ballet skirts and the clowns clad in motley and the animal handlers with tiny chainnecked capuchins on their shoulders. The freakshow clung to the tent walls, their obligations already fulfilled within the preshow tents on the road to the big top. He found his place among the crowd and scanned their sullen faces. An albino with pale coiled hair shaped like the fronds of a tree watched through a tiny fluttering gap in the inner tentwall. Beyond the flap, the ringmaster in his smooth voice announced the acts of the night. The albino stood beside a three hundred pound woman whose arms and legs were turning to stone. She sighed and looked at the grassy earth beneath. Her limbs wrinkled and elephantine, cast in amber beneath the candystripe canvas. Beside her, a seven foot and five inch tall man, the Eight Foot Man, paced around on legs that looked brand new to him. He said something to himself that no one could hear.

A clown bounced around, loosing his arms at the threshold of the ring. Another behind him smoked. The ringmaster's microphone squealed inside the ring. He said Prepare to be delighted, stupefied, terrified, thrilled. He said you will see men and ladies come closer to death than perhaps you thought imaginable. He said Hold onto your seats and let the show commence.

Woodard moved to the canopy wall and yanked up on a tassled rope, which pulled up the wallflap, and beneath it a horde of baroque executants of every type flooded in. Two showgirls named Barbara and Alice sallied out into the ring center in shimmering swinging outfits, their legs prancing and toned. Behind them, two elephants loped in thundering circles. From just outside the tent, a man named Croll kicked his motorcycle into gear and tore through the backstage, sliding with spraddled legs through the mud, fishtail tracks in his wake. The embroidery on the back of his jacket read Croll the Great. He tore in a circle around the elephants, who lumbered counterclockwise in tight rings, their aged cracked skin shifting loosely with every step, their ears swinging like saloon doors, their eyes leaking odd runny tears.

A moment of this and Croll the Great stands on the seat of his cycle, his arms outstretched, leaning rightward in a circle. A lap or two and Bobo the elephant kneels and Barbara steps up onto his trunk, her pearly smile wrapped in red lipstick. She too casts her arms out to either side as Bobo lifts his head and stumbles to his feet and suddenly she is thrust heavenward, the audience gasping and cheering. Beneath, Croll takes a seat on the bike and roars out of the tent. A stagehand named Besser seizes the other elephant's halter and guides him to center stage beside Bobo, where Alice the showgirl strokes his trunk and he submits, lowering his head for her to climb aboard. She does, and the elephant lifts her to his back. The crowd roars and then Alice taps him on the back and he begins tilting forward. And the crowd must think something is about to go wrong, for they quiet. The elephant shifts his weight to his front until he is propped up entirely on his forelegs, his pillarlike hind legs in the air behind him, Alice standing on his rump, egging him on.

The crowd cheers and the elephant lowers itself once again. Barbara teeters to the middle of the elephant's back, and Alice does the same, directly opposite her. She looks at Barbara and Barbara nods a little nod and they turn to face away from one another, wobbling a little on the spines of the beasts, and they stretch their dainty fingers high above them. Then they lean back and point their legs forward in unison and flip back, each to the other's place, stockinged legs arcing, curled hair hurled centripetally about.

When had the music begun? In this age the orchestra had been done away with, replaced by a recorded horn or horns playing Fucik beneath the stands. He watched the elephants. African Bush elephants, bought as infants from a decrepit zoo somewhere. Ohio or Kansas. One of the Dakotas. They walked in more circles, the beauties barelegged atop them.

At this time he would retreat into the night air and strip and don his uniform, a clownish orange vest and bowler cap atop a brownplaid suitset. He did this and jogged across the lawn, digging through his pockets for his truck keys. He found them and opened the driver's door of his boxtruck at the edge of the lot. He climbed inside. Felt the weight of her shifting in the trailer.

He drove the truck across the lawn and backed it to an opening on the ring's other side. He got out and peered inside the backroom on this side. There was no one. Then he hefted the keys until he found the right one and unlocked the trunk door. Gonna be waiting for us, he said to the bear.

She paced in tiny circles, the cage only twice her size. Two hundred pounds and declawed. He opened the door to her cage and slipped a leash and muzzle over her. Months of practice and he could secure them around her head in two motions. Five seconds of danger. He pulled her from the cage and then stepped down and yanked a set of wooden steps onto the ground below. She walked down them and stood.

Pete, Pete, he called to the tent. In a moment a short Italian appeared in the threshold. Gimme a hand, Woodard said. Bring the rod.

Pete nodded and disappeared. Woodard stood out there in the dark with the bear. She huffed dully. Strange sight we are, he said. A dimly lit man stopped along a path across the river to stare at him.

Pete appeared with the rod. He made a wide circle around the creature and handed it to Woodard. There were little jester bells on the ends of the collar and they tinkled as she walked. He looked at the rod. On the end of it were two prongs. You keep that in hand, said Pete. He had a small lisp. Don't trust that damned thing.

Woodard walked the bear to the tent edge and led her inside and waited in the tiny room. Put a conical birthday hat on her. Waited for his cue.

The end of Entry of the Gladiators. The final strings collided in tremolo with the horns rising and constant and triumphant, and the final resonance sounded, and for a moment all who were there are on their feet, the elephants are chauffeured out the rear entrance opposite and Pete rushes to the stage dragging a tricycle behind him and

Woodard brings her to the fore. The ringmaster says Give em a big hand, ladies and gentlemen. The grizzly's stalking steps lead her just before the crowd, and they are clapping and shrinking. One of the children lets out a terrifying cry. But the bear is unleashed and sits back on her hind legs and lifts her paws into the air before her and applauds, and the crowd matches her, laughing and whooping, and the crying is silenced. Woodard, rod in hand, bows, and when he does she does too.

They walk backward, the bear on four feet again, and he motions to the tricycle. She climbs aboard and rides the thing crudely in wobbling circles around the ring. The din of the crowd has become deafening. When the bear passes Woodard he can hear the little bells around her neck ringing flat and pitiful. Her little jowls hanging and dripping white saliva. For a moment he sees the whites of her eyes. Tiny childlike eyes. Was she looking at him?

And now what? She rides the bike at him. A horrible childish vision, a feverish dream. She tumbles off the back of the bike and onto her feet and lopes her way to him. He looks at the crowd and half of them are looking at the bear and the other at him, as if to discern whether this is part of the act. But his face resolves that mystery. He hefts the rod in his hand and touches the button on its side with his thumb. He presses it and the current within the rod pops to life. Now now, he says to himself. Had he heard someone somewhere say that? Get back over there, he said, too low for the bear to hear. Her tongue lolling. Ambling closer.

Out in the room beyond, the crew and the talent have huddled together around the albino, the fat woman and the Eight Foot Man and the trapeze artists and the girls staring mouths agape through the open doorway. Pete has commenced drinking and stares wetlipped through a gap in the shoulders of those before him. The clown stands behind him and keeps whispering past his shoulder. What's happening now? he asks. Barbara takes a stepladder and

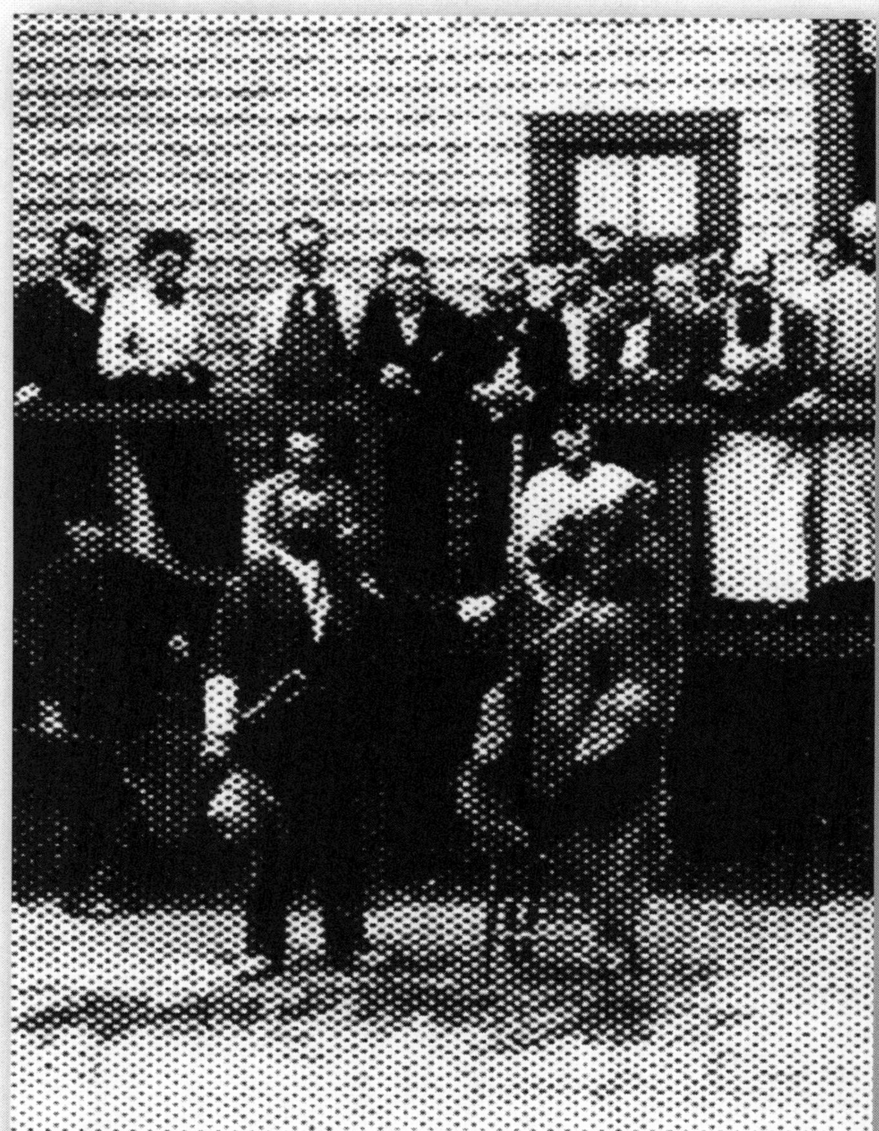

pushes it past the gathering to the middle of the inner tentwall, which is suspended on a line eight feet above the ground. From here she can see the place entire. The look in Woodard's eyes and the trembling in his extremities. The calm way the bear approaches. He winds up and thumps the thing broadside with the rod and there is a silence. The bear stops and and looks up at him. Some of the women have clashed their hands over their mouths. Then one of the men pierces the silence. Shock the damn thing, he shouts, and the crowd claps uproariously. Woodard takes his eyes from her for a moment to watch them. They are there and they have paid twenty dollars apiece for the show. There will be acts to follow, clowns and swinging trapeze artists and illusionists and capuchin monkeys atop shoulders. Tomorrow the paper will come out, its review written by one of the anonymous faces watching this ominous spectacle roll out. Its headline will read Zambelli Circus Brings Fearful Sights, Crowds Delighted. His fearlessness will earn him a slap on the back.

He takes a step back and when he does the bear follows after. The crowd is now screaming, jumping and stamping, the children with bloodlust in their tiny eyes, the men red and feverish, the women peeking between their fingers. He thumps the thing on the side again, this time harder, and it huffs and shakes its head and keeps walking. He grips the rod and the bear looks off in the direction of the tricycle and perhaps she has changed direction but it is too late. He has thrust the twopronged rod into the flesh above her shoulder and her reaction is instant. She shakes her head and rears back a moment, the fearsome creature she perhaps once was for a mere second visible, and then she falls back to her four feet, and tosses her head around. Woodard climbs atop her and clips the leash to her bellcollar once more and drags her out of the tent.

Bears' eyes, like humans', flit about in something resembling REM sleep. Their lips twitch and their limbs move. They can be startled awake without notice or apparent stimulus, and have been observed waking panicked and looking for some unseen threat, growling in their empty burrows. She too may have been dreaming. About what?

Long ago she had plodded along the hillside behind her mother, the potentilla stirring beneath a roiling drystorm. Bison in their numbers grazed stilly off in the flatlands like geologic features. Two more cubs plodded behind her, chasing each other. On the ground below, families pulled their cars to the side to take photos of them.

Hours later and the night had fallen. They slept on the ground some place while the lightning burned fractalous through the black. A crack of thunder exploded through the universe. She laid there with her eyes open. Her mother breathed gently. The storm moved away, pulsing lights miles off. She fell asleep. A soft rumble across the taiga. The soft wind singing wistful. The firs shimmying, rocking, like ritual dancers, their movements demonstrated in empty vacuous night.

He couldn't sleep. He looked at the bedside clock. Three thirteen. He threw off the blankets and stood and pulled his pants back on. He went to the kitchen and pulled a can of Wolf brand chili from the cupboard and poured it into a pot and watched it bubble on the stovetop. He poured the chili into a bowl and sat slumped on the recliner. Turned on the television and groaned and looked over the his shoulder at the refrigerator. Grunted. Then he stood and got a soda from it and sat back down. Poker was on. He switched through the channels. Cooking and jewelry sales and infomercials about a strange object of unknown

purpose. My life has never been the same, said the woman holding it.
The night quiet, as if it were holding its breath. Waiting for him to make some move. He walked through the trailer park and up to the big top. In a few days it would be gone. He ducked inside and found a flashlight in the back room and flicked it on and ducked into the grand room, swinging the beam up to the corners of the tent where it rippled lightly like the last thing in a forgotten place. The bleachers stood the same, covered in discarded refuse of popcorn and pretzel ends and plastic beer cups and cotton candy cones. The grass around the rings trampled and torn.
He went out and up past the elephant truck, a semi with tiny windows barred and locked. A painting of a clown face and the words The Great Zambelli Circus on its side. He tried to hear them stir but they didn't. Just past them sat the bear truck. He fumbled in his pockets and came out with the trailer keys and opened the door and she was there, lying on her side, a mass of dark fur. It smelled like old shit. Like a horse stall. The shit was matted in her fur. She yawned, her great yellowtoothed mouth strung up with saliva. Fresh sores shown like plasmic calderas on her skin. Hey, he muttered. Got something for you.
He went to the passenger seat and opened an Igloo cooler atop it. He brought it back and opened it. Well, he said. It ain't much. The bear looked at him with her child's eyes. He threw the meat in the cage and she leaned and licked it up off the floor. How's that, he asked. I prefer it grilled myself.
He watched her chew, her giant jaws hinging and yawning. He threw another slab to her, the last in the cooler. He closed it and set it on the ground and then sat on it. What was that about today? he asked. He squinted at her. She was sitting, her mouth hanging limply. Don't feel like talking? Well. Just tell me you won't do it again.
He watched her for a moment. She stared at the cooler. Ain't got nothin in it, he said. He stood and opened it and showed

her. A little watery blood pooled in the corner. She sat there. Then she laid down. Well, he said. Good night. You're pretty strange, you know that? He closed the doors and locked them.

The lights lowered and the ringmaster Beale called out over the microphone. Ladies and gentlemen, boys and girls, he called. Hold onto your hats and cling to the edges of your seats. Prepare to be delighted, stupefied, terrified, thrilled.
The children silenced and their parents pointed at the man, whispering Shhh. Between the ringmaster's declarations children chewed buttered popcorn. Slurped at the dregs of soda cups. Soon, continued the ringmaster, you will see men and ladies come closer to death than perhaps you thought imaginable.
You will see fantastical beasts the likes of which can be found nowhere else on this continent, and laugh your pants off at our troupe of hilarious clowns.
Pete was on the other side of the tent's back room. Laugh your pants off, he said. What the hell?
Beale the ringmaster asked for a big round of applause. From inside the backroom the applause was like a stampede. Shit, said Woodard. They bus people in?
He peered out the flap. Men and women sat on the bleacher steps and stood in the space beside the stands. Tiny children sat atop their fathers' shoulders, their little hands clutching the thinning hair. He closed the flap.
Gene. Gene, Barbara said. He looked at her. Her eyes were wide. He hadn't seen her. The rope, she said.
Damn, he said. He stood and ran to the golden rope and yanked up on it. The troupe had assembled while he was sitting. He hadn't noticed. The girls ran out followed by the elephants and Croll ripped through the walls on his bike. Woodard ran out to the truck, fumbling through his pocket for the keys. When he got to the truck he pounded with his

fist on the closed back door. It's show time, he yelled. He climbed in the driver's seat and backed up to the tent. Pete was in the doorway looking out. The evening sky had turned a deep indigo, the tone of late August nights.
Woodard climbed down from the truck and unlocked the trailer door. The hinges groaned with the weight of the doors. The bear blinked in the light. She was laying on the truck floor, her legs splayed in four directions on the cool metal. The trailer reeked and flies buzzed past Woodards ears in little doppler circles.
Come on now, said Woodard. He unlocked her cage. Can I see that leash, he yelled to Pete.
Pete ducked inside and then reappeared and ran it to him. He opened the cagedoor and tried to slip it over her massive head, draping it over her snout, his arm bent carefully inside the cage. Her pulled back but the leashloop caught on her jaw. She balked, shaking her head. Come on, said Woodard.
He tried it again. The loop fell over her mouth and when he pulled on it it went up over the crown of her head. Dammit, he said.
We got to go, said Pete.
She won't move her head.
They're waiting.
I'm not opening this door unless she's got a leash on her.
Why?
Cause she's a bear.
You think the leash is going to stop her from attacking you?
Gonna stop her from getting away. Attacking someone else.
Let me see that.
Pete moved over and reached inside. He grabbed the leashloop and set it over the bear's mouth and smacked its jowls twice.
Get your damn head up, he said.
You're a dumbass, said Woodard.
Well we're both out here putting a dog collar on a bear aren't we?

15

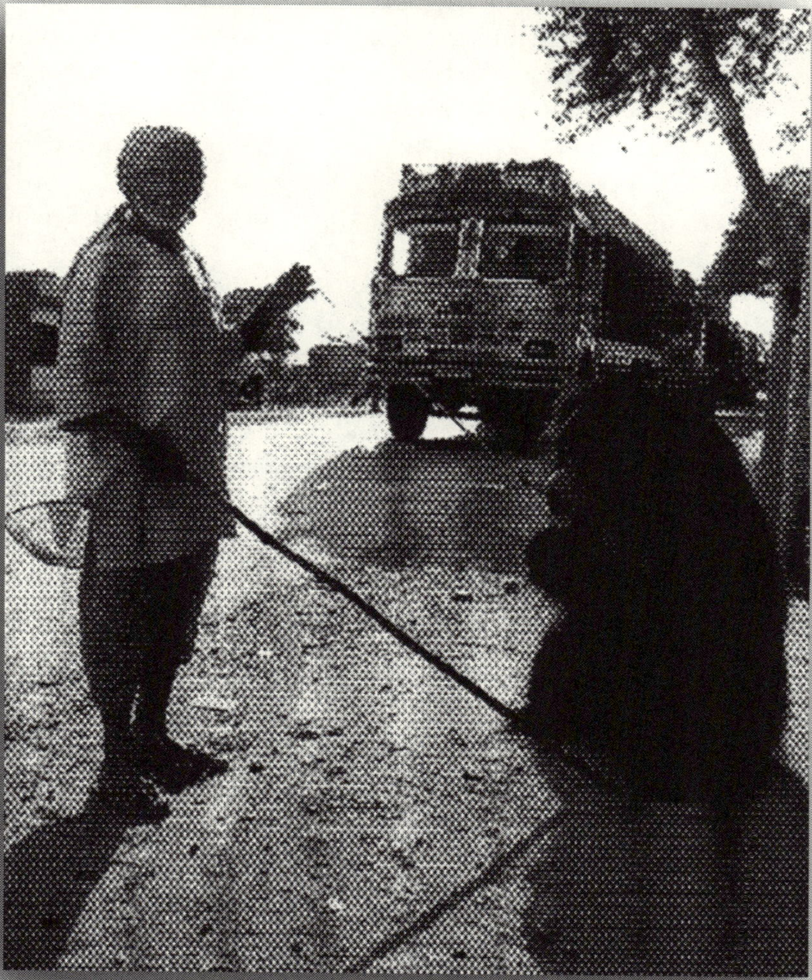

Woodard spat.

Pete said Come on you damn thing. A stagehand with an accent came out from the tent and said Gene, they are waiting for you. Then he disappeared.

Come on, now, said Woodard to Pete.

She don't wanna, grunted Pete. He jerked the collar up over the bear's head.

I'll tell you what, said Woodard. He didn't finish. When Pete turned around he was running into the tent and then emerging with the pointed rod. He pressed the button on the side of it and the current within it buzzed alive. We got ten seconds, said Woodard.

I almost got it, said Pete.

Move over.

Woodard sidled beside him and threw open the trailer doors. The bear was looking up at him. He grabbed the leash loop and fitted it over her snout. Last chance, he said. He pulled up on the leash. The bear groaned and turned her head manic. He tried and failed to get the loop over her. She growled deep and for a moment he stepped back and forgot to breathe. The awesome power of it. The horrible depth of the cry. She stayed lying down, her mouth stretched open, banded together by shaking ropes of saliva.

He stepped forward and thrust the rod into the flesh above her shoulder. At once she cried and leaned her great head back. The skin beneath her hide twitched. Do it now, said Woodard. Do it now. Pete rushed forward and stretched the leash over her great yawning skull and tightened the loop. Woodard ran to the side of the trailer and stuck the rod through the bars into the flesh of her haunch and she leapt up and Pete yanked on the leash and she stumbled stupidly onto the earth.

When he led the creature into the tent the crowd looked as though they had been waiting some time for him. He guided her to the tentcenter and unclipped the leash from the collar. All that only to remove it once more.

The bear walked to the tricycle and mounted it and rode it around in pathetic circles. She was not wearing her frilled neckwear or her birthday party cap. He looked once more at the crowd, and while some stood and clapped others sat transfixed, their hands to their faces. Had they seen such a thing before? A creaking rotation squealed from the pedals of the trike, accompanied by calliope music playing on a loop.

Round she went, and round again. Her hands hung limply over the handlebars and her mouth hung open. A string of saliva ran down from her panting tongue. He had forgotten to put the muzzle on her. He reached in his pocket and touched the muzzle fabric. Shit, he muttered.

Two more circles on the trike and the audience had taken their seats again. He motioned to the bear and she dismounted and followed him to the center of the ring. Woodard put his hands in the air and hopped, and the bear did the same.

The crowd erupted. Woodard jumped, each time spinning a little. Pete rolled a hula hoop into the ring. Woodard grabbed it and motioned with it oddly to the bear, who stood wobbling on her hind legs. He moved his head in rotations of the neck, and soon the bear also moved her head as such. He placed the hula hoop around her neck where it swung in circles. She was looking at him, her head rocking slightly. He looked at her chest, raised up to him unnaturally. She stepped back and forth. The crowd was laughing and clapping. He felt the muzzle again in his pocket. Come on now, he said. Just a minute more.

Out of the tentwalls came another hula hoop and then another, three rings spinning concentric from her neck. After a moment Woodard reached up and grabbed them and rolled them backstage. She thumped back down to her fours, wandering around the ring dully. Hey, he said. Come on. We aren't done yet. He whacked her on the belly. Get up, up. She stood again and he went behind her.

Pete came out with a checkered flag and a starter pistol and Woodard lined up in place beside her. He stood and crouched in a runner's stance. The bear did the same. The gun went off and Woodard ran, rod in hand, in dramatized form around the ring. The bear hobbled beside him. The crowd whooped and cheered. Woodard mocked panting, and the bear took the lead. Woodard regained his position, the bear behind him. They had run half of the ring. In the second half of the ring Woodard pretended to trip, and when be rose again the bear was nearing Pete, who held the flag high in the air. Woodard got to his feet, the crowd jumping and cheering for the bear. He ran and doubled over exhausted feet before Pete, who waved the flag behind the bear.
Woodard breathed hard. He paced around, his hands on his sides. The bear put her hands in the air. The crowd was raucous.
And as quickly as they cheered they screamed. He doubled over to mime breathing and saw her mass of brown fur bounding in a blur toward him, her huge mouth the last thing he saw before he was on the ground. She reared up on her legs and threw her arms atop him. He crumpled under her weight and his head slammed against the floor. She scraped at him with the places where her claws once were, and then took his orange shirt and overalls between her teeth and picked him up, slamming and wiping him against the vinyl. Woodard screamed. In the corners of his vision he could see indistinct figures hurrying about, hands to mouths, kicking the bear's back or wailing.
He felt her teeth dig into the flesh of his breast. He grabbed her chest fur and pushed against it, the hair coarse and salivadripped. She felt like she might have been a man in a costume. He pulled his knees up and tried to wiggle free but her weight was too great. She grabbed his arm and he could hear it cracking in her jaws. He yelled until his voice cracked and nothing came from him but a croak. Warm blood ran from his arm and chest.

She puffed and roared into him, cables of spit snapping forth from her jaws. He looked down at her and his eyes were as wide as he could make them. His arms taut and sinewy pushed against her. The rod had fallen from his grasp.
For a moment the creature released him and looked behind her. When she turned back the two stared each at the other. Her eyes were tiny, watery. As if what she was doing pained even her. Slivers of white at the iris's edge. The product of fifty million years. Was there some recognition there? Pinhole pupils met his gaze. He couldn't breathe.
Two men grabbed him from his armpits and pulled him up. He looked up at them and then at the animal. She was jerking her head against his, whipping her skull to and fro. He made sounds unknown to him, wheezing and panting and struggling. The bears neck jerked up and her maw was dripping with his blood. He looked at his shoulder, the orange of the overalls doused in red. He hadn't felt her bite him.
She reeled and twitched, howling. Someone had stabbed the pronged rod into her. He watched her jump back. She squirmed, batting her paws before her face. Someone asked Woodard if he was okay. He heard someone say Hold his neck closed. What? he said. What? No one answered him.
He tried to get up but his arm failed him. A crowd of people now gathered around him and held their sweaters to his neck. The showgirls cried. The bear jumped and fell. Pete had managed to get the leash around her and was shocking the bear repeatedly. Her head darted around, legions of foreign glances cast upon her. Her fecescrusted hide undulating like a carpet.
Are you okay? someone asked him.
Yes. Yes I'm okay, he said. He didn't know why he said it. He didn't know why they asked.
Out in the audience spectators were grabbing up their children and making for the exits. Women cried and men covered their children's eyes and rushed from the place, while the act entire swirled around the horror. He was sweating.

The world turning white. He could feel his blood pooling on the mat beneath him. A noise rose within him, a humming. He listened to it. Foreign figures twirled above him. He could feel them picking him up and carrying him somewhere. He wiped his forehead and panted.

They took the bear and locked her in the truck without food or water until the morning. When they walked away she was whining inside the trailer. She walked in tiny circles in the darkened cage, her cries unheard. The big top was empty. In the morning the papers would read Circus Bear Fatally Mauls Trainer, and he'd be buried some place nearby. And after reading the paper someone in the circus crew will drag the muzzled creature from its cage out onto the esplanade and tie its leash to a tree and then shoot the thing, born thousands of miles distant, of a creature long forgotten. She'll roar and yank on the leash as the shot enters her chest once and again, and then she'll flop to the earth panting, drooling, mouth open, tongue lolling. In a minute she'll go limp. Her last mewling breath will leave her. Her eyes will flare and then freeze. Her last sight the tent city, the cars and the passersby within them slowing to watch.

Made in United States
Orlando, FL
16 October 2023